Food We Eat

Then and Now

Debbie Croft

Contents

Eating Habits Over the Years 2
Family Food in the Early 1900s 3
Food From the 1950s Onwards 8
Food Today 12
Many Foods to Choose 23
How to Make a Couscous Salad 24
Glossary 31
Index 32

Eating Habits Over the Years

The types of foods that people include in their diets have changed over the past hundred years. Today, a greater variety of foods is eaten. Most of the foods that were eaten in the past are still available and continue to be eaten today. However, a wider **range** of products has slowly been introduced.

Families today enjoy tasting and sharing many different foods.

Family Food in the Early 1900s

During the first half of the twentieth century, people mainly ate very simple foods that could be grown at home or **purchased** at small, local grocery shops. These shops provided only basic foods.

Many families had a vegetable garden in their backyard where they grew food such as carrots, beans, tomatoes, cucumbers and pumpkins. Some people grew fruit trees, which **bore** lemons and oranges, or stone fruits, such as peaches and apricots.

People spent a lot of time taking care of the family vegetable garden.

Think and Talk About ...

Sometimes, people exchanged fruit and vegetables with their neighbours.

During the early 1900s, people often made butter using the cream that floated to the top of the milk. Some families milked cows on their farms; others bought milk from the milkman, and had it delivered by horse and cart early each morning. Women sometimes made their own bread, but some families purchased loaves of freshly baked bread from the baker, who also delivered supplies every day.

Think and Talk About ...

Homemade butter was made by beating cream or using a butter **churn**.

Churning butter requires time and energy, but only simple equipment.

Many people ate beef and lamb from animals killed on their farms. Chicken was considered a **delicacy**, so it was only eaten on special occasions. People kept chickens so they would have eggs to eat.

Before people began working in many different industries, lots of families had small farms to grow what they needed.

People who lived in town bought meat in very small quantities, as most homes did not have a refrigerator. Some had an **ice chest** that contained a large block of ice, which was delivered by a local supplier. But when the weather was very hot, the ice melted after only one day. Food could not be kept cold for long, so it was often eaten the same day it was bought. When refrigerators became available, people began to shop less often, because food could be stored safely for a longer period of time.

This ice chest is from sometime around 1900.

People bought other basic food items, such as sugar, tea and flour, at local shops. Even without refrigerators, these foods could be kept at home, as they did not spoil. Most women stayed at home during the day. They used wood ovens to bake bread, cakes and biscuits using simple ingredients.

Baking bread takes a long time. First the dough is kneaded, then left to rise and finally it is baked in the oven.

Think and Talk About ...

Food items such as sugar and tea were **rationed** in many countries during the war years of the early 1940s.

Food From the 1950s Onwards

During the second half of the twentieth century, people began to enjoy a wider range of foods as part of their diet. When supermarkets were introduced, people **relied** on these large shops to provide the foods they wanted for their families. They were no longer **restricted** to eating foods that were grown locally. Supermarkets were able to obtain foods from other areas and transport them to towns and cities all over the country.

Supermarkets changed the way people shopped, as they could get most of the things they needed from one place.

However, people continued to eat foods that were simple to cook and readily available to buy. For dinner at night, many families ate beef, lamb, pork or chicken, which was often grilled or roasted. A main meal usually included potatoes, one green vegetable (peas, beans or spinach) and one orange vegetable (carrot or pumpkin). These were either boiled or baked. In summer, salad vegetables, such as lettuce, tomato and cucumber were eaten.

Throughout time, families have often enjoyed catching up over dinner.

Think and Talk About ...

In the 1950s and 1960s, most foods were cooked at home, not **processed** in factories.

Refrigerators and Freezers

The development of household refrigerators and freezers allowed people to buy and store foods safely. Cold or frozen food could be kept and used at a later date.

This photograph is from a 1960s advertising campaign for refrigerators.

Trucks with refrigerated trailers are now used to transport a huge variety of goods to local supermarkets. Fresh supplies are delivered every day in most parts of the country.

As soon as fresh supplies arrive at the supermarket, they need to be unpacked and put on the shelves.

Food Today

The development of a modern **multicultural** society has provided families with the opportunity to taste a wide variety of foods. People who arrive from other countries bring with them their own knowledge about the foods their families eat and enjoy. When restaurants are opened in towns and cities, different varieties of foods are served and new eating **experiences** are provided for customers.

Advertising also helps people learn more about different foods that can be bought and places where they can eat. Sometimes, families visit a new restaurant to eat there or purchase takeaway food. At other times, they buy foods that they have never tried before from supermarkets. People have become more **experimental** with the foods they prepare and eat.

In many cities, people can walk down the street and taste food from all over the world.

Big supermarkets offer a wide range of products to choose from.

Supermarkets

In recent years, many different foods have been introduced to our supermarkets. People are encouraged to try these new products through various forms of advertising. News reports also explain the health **benefits** of some of these foods.

Some of the newer foods available in our supermarkets include different types of fruits, vegetables, grains and seeds.

Think and Talk About ...

With the use of modern technology, busy families can place supermarket orders online and have food delivered to their homes.

Olives

Olives are the fruit from olive trees. Olives range in colour from a yellowish-green to purple or black. Green olives are picked when they have grown to full size, but before they have started to ripen. Other olives are picked at the beginning of the ripening cycle and range from green to a red or brown colour. Olives that are fully ripe are purple, brown or black.

Olive trees grow well in places with cool winters and hot, dry summers.

Sometimes, the seeds from green olives are removed and the fruit is filled with the red, juicy flesh of the pimiento, or chilli pepper. This gives the olive a slightly sweeter flavour, rather than its usual salty taste.

Olives can be eaten on their own as a snack, or as part of a savoury dish.

Olive oil is believed to have more health properties than other types of oil.

Think and Talk About ...

Olives are pressed to produce olive oil.

Sun-Dried Tomatoes

Sun-dried tomatoes are ripe tomatoes that have been dried in the sun. Usually, it takes from four to ten days in the sun for the tomatoes to lose their moisture. Even when the tomatoes have been dried, they do not lose their nutritional **value**.

Tomatoes of all shapes, colours and varieties can be dried. In Italy, people often dry tomatoes in the sun on the roofs of their houses. Because of their high water content, tomatoes spoil very quickly unless they are preserved in some way.

Today, sun-dried tomatoes are often preserved in olive oil, with a combination of herbs, such as rosemary, basil and garlic.

Special racks can be used to dry large quantities of tomatoes in the sun.

Fresh tomatoes lose about 90% of their weight in the drying process.

Kale

Kale is a vegetable that has green or purple leaves. It is related to the wild cabbage. The most common variety is curly kale, which is mostly sold in bunches. Sometimes, loose leaves of baby kale are available in supermarkets.

Kale is very high in nutrients and is easy to grow. Seeds are planted in autumn and continue to grow through winter, often surviving harsh frosts.

Kale is a good source of vitamin C and calcium.

Grown around the world, kale forms part of many countries' traditional dishes.

Celeriac

Celeriac is a variety of celery, and is often called celery root. It consists of a round, brown root with long, green leaves. Only the root is eaten. The skin is peeled from the root, and the flesh inside is crisp and white.

Celeriac can be eaten raw in salads. Sometimes, it is boiled or steamed, or added to soups and casseroles. It can also be mashed or puréed.

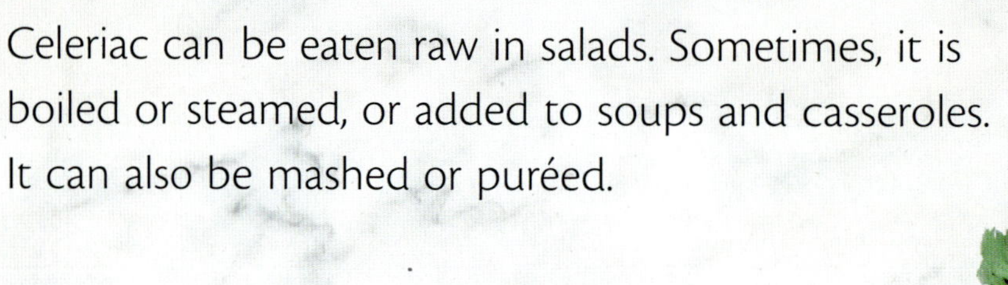

Celeriac is widely available and usually at its best during the cooler months.

People eat celeriac because it is low in fat and a good source of vitamin B.

Quinoa

Quinoa (pronounced *keen-wah*) is a grain crop that is grown for its seeds. These seeds are an excellent source of protein, iron and fibre. The whole grains have a slightly nutty flavour.

Quinoa seeds are mostly white, but they can also be red or black. Quinoa comes from South America and is becoming popular all over the world. Sometimes, it is used to replace rice, or mixed with rice, in a recipe.

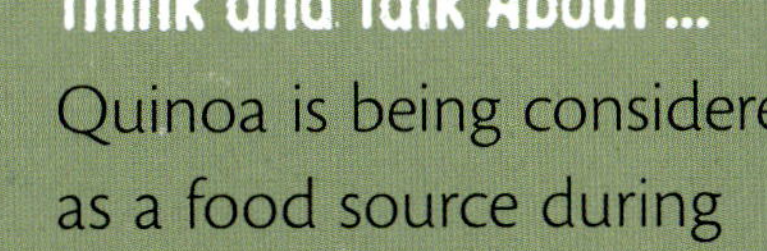

Think and Talk About ...

Quinoa is being considered as a food source during long-term space flights.

South American people have eaten quinoa for thousands of years.

People prepare quinoa to eat by washing and then boiling it.

Couscous

Couscous is a product made from wheat. It is traditionally cooked by steaming. Instant couscous, which has been pre-steamed and dried, is cooked by simply pouring boiling water over the grains and allowing them to absorb the moisture.

Originally, couscous was eaten in North Africa. However, its quick and easy preparation methods have made it a very popular dish in many countries around the world.

Often, couscous is served with a meat or vegetable stew spooned over the cooked grains. It can also be combined with vegetables and made into a healthy salad.

Couscous is made from semolina grains.

In parts of North Africa and the Middle East, couscous is a staple food.

Pumpkin Seeds

Pumpkin seeds are also known as "pepitas". They are flat, dark-green seeds with a nutty flavour. Pepitas are an excellent source of minerals essential for a healthy body.

Often, pumpkin seeds are added to breakfast cereal and vegetable dishes, sprinkled on salads, or ground and added to burgers.

People eat pumpkin seeds because they are high in protein and iron.

Pumpkin seeds can be eaten roasted and spiced as a snack, or raw in muesli.

Tofu

Tofu, or bean curd, is a product made from soy milk. It is very popular in East and South East Asia. Tofu has a subtle flavour and can be used in sweet or savoury dishes.

Tofu is rich in protein and replaces meat in many vegetarian diets. The two main types of tofu are silken (or soft) and firm.

Soybeans are soaked in water, crushed and boiled to get soy milk, which is made into tofu.

Tofu can replace meat in a tasty skewer.

Many Foods to Choose

Over time, the range of foods available has influenced the food choices made by families.

These days, many people have access to technology and knowledge of healthy foods. They also live in multicultural societies. These factors encourage people to select a wide range of foods to enjoy every day.

People like shopping at big markets to get fresh produce and food from different cultures.

How to Make a Couscous Salad

Goal: To make a couscous salad

Ingredients:

- 200 grams of instant couscous

- 200 millilitres of vegetable stock

- two tablespoons of olive oil
- two spring onions

- one yellow capsicum

Important!
Ask an adult to help you with this procedure.

- 30 grams of sun-dried tomatoes

- one small cucumber

- 50 grams of feta cheese

- two tablespoons of lemon juice

- two tablespoons of flat-leaf parsley

- three tablespoons of toasted pine nuts

Equipment:

- two bowls – one large and one small
- a small saucepan

- a tablespoon
- plastic food wrap
- a sharp knife

- a chopping board
- a fork
- a serving platter

Steps:

1. Place the couscous in a large bowl.
2. Pour the stock and one tablespoon of olive oil into a saucepan. Heat the mixture on the stove until it just begins to boil.
3. Remove the mixture from the heat and pour it over the couscous. Cover the bowl of couscous with plastic food wrap and leave it to stand for about 10 minutes.

4. Finely chop the spring onions. Use the green stem as well as the white bulb of the plant.
5. Remove the stem and seeds from the capsicum using the knife. Cut the flesh into thin strips.

6. Roughly chop the sun-dried tomatoes into small pieces.

7. **Rinse** the cucumber and then cut it in half lengthways. Cut each half lengthways again to make four long pieces. Chop the pieces of cucumber into small chunks.

8. Lightly **crumble** the feta cheese using your fingers.

9. Uncover the couscous when it is completely cold. Use a fork to separate the grains.

10. Add the chopped spring onions, capsicum, sun-dried tomatoes, cucumber and crumbled cheese to the couscous.

11. Combine the remaining olive oil and the lemon juice in the small bowl. Add the mixture to the couscous in the large bowl. Gently stir to mix all the ingredients together.

12. Arrange the couscous mixture on a serving platter.
13. Roughly chop the parsley. Mix with the toasted pine nuts and sprinkle over the couscous salad before serving.

Glossary

benefits *(noun)*	advantages
bore *(past-tense verb)*	produced or yielded
churn *(noun)*	a container used to turn milk or cream into butter
crumble *(present-tense verb)*	break into smaller pieces
delicacy *(noun)*	a luxury or treat
experiences *(noun)*	events or happenings
experimental *(adjective)*	likely to try new things
ice chest *(noun)*	a box that uses ice to keep food cold
multicultural *(adjective)*	made up of people from different cultures
processed *(past-tense verb)*	treated and made into something else
purchased *(past-tense verb)*	bought
range *(noun)*	variety or choice
rationed *(past-tense verb)*	only a small amount was allowed
relied *(past-tense verb)*	trusted or depended
restricted *(past-tense verb)*	limited
rinse *(present-tense verb)*	wash with water
value *(noun)*	worth or importance

Index

advertising 10, 12, 13
bread 4, 7
butter 4, 31
celeriac 18
chicken 5, 9
cooking 9, 20, 24–30
couscous 20, 24–30
eggs 5
frozen 10
fruit 3, 13, 14, 15
growing 3, 5, 8, 14, 17, 19
health benefits 13
health 13, 15, 20, 21, 23
ice chest 6, 31
kale 17
meat 5, 6, 9, 20, 22
milk 4, 22, 31
minerals 21
multicultural 12, 23, 31
nutrients 17
nutritional value 16
olive oil 15, 16, 24, 27, 30
olives 14–15
pumpkin seeds 21
quinoa 19
range 2, 8, 13, 23, 31
refrigerator 6, 7, 10
restaurant 12
shopping 3, 6, 7, 8, 23
sun-dried tomatoes 16, 25, 28, 29
supermarket 8, 11, 12, 13, 17
tofu 22
transport 8, 11
vegetables 3, 9, 13, 17, 20
vitamins 17, 18